© 1994 Sigrid Heuck (Text)
© 1994 Bernhard Oberdieck (Art)
© 1994 Annick Press (English edition)
© 1992 by K. Thienemanns Verlag, Stuttgart-Wien (original edition)
Translation: Anne W. Millyard
Cover design: Sheryl Shapiro

Annick Press Ltd.

Canadian Cataloguing in Publication Data

Heuck, Sigrid
  A ghost in the castle

ISBN 1-55037-328-5 (bound) ISBN 1-55037-331-5 (pbk.)

I. Oberdieck, Bernhard. II. Title.

PZ7.H438 1993 j833'.914 C93-093660-4

The text of this book has been set in Garamond by Attic Typesetting.

Distributed in Canada by:
Firefly Books Ltd.
250 Sparks Avenue
Willowdale, Ontario M2H 2S4

Distributed in the U.S.A. by:
Firefly Books (U.S.) Inc.
P.O. Box 1325
Ellicott Station
Buffalo, New York 14205

Printed and bound in Hong Kong
by Book Art Inc., Toronto

A Ghost in the Castle

Story by Sigrid Heuck
Art by Bernard Oberdieck

Annick Press

Once upon a time, long ago, there was a white owl.

It belonged to a small circus that travelled from town to town.

Wherever the circus stopped and the big tent went up, tickets sold out very quickly. The marching brass band invited everyone to forget troublesome thoughts, and to join the parade.

The townspeople admired the fearless acrobats doing headstands on horseback and the splits on the high wire. The clowns tripped over one another's big feet and people laughed until tears ran down their cheeks. They even liked the smell of the sawdust.

Their favourite part, however, was the animal show. People fed the elephant, took rides on the camel, teased the monkeys, talked to the parrot, patted the little pony—and stood clear of the tiger cage: they were very afraid of the great beast. And they looked in awe at the rare owl.

The children would stare at her dignified, motionless body, waiting for her to blink just once and prove that she was alive.

And blink she would. The children cheered. But at night, when the townspeople had gone home, there would erupt from her cage a long, mournful sound, mysterious and lonely all at once: "Whooooo-Whooooo!"

The owl had been confined to her cage for so long that she couldn't remember seeing other white owls, and didn't even know that she could fly. She had no idea how it would feel to spread her wings wide and sail in silvery moonlight across the countryside while most other living creatures were asleep. And, as food was brought to her each day, she had never learned to catch a mouse.

Now, the person in charge of the circus was a greedy man, who was always grumbling about having no money. Therefore, when one day there was a knock on the door and a stranger offered to purchase the owl, the circus man was tempted.

"What do you want her for?" he asked.

"I tend the gardens of a very rich man, whose castle has been haunted by unsettling sounds at night," said the stranger. "In the attic can be heard scratches, squeaks, whistles and a hundred tiny rattles, keeping everyone awake. Even the footmen are frightened. I seem to be the only one who realizes what sort of 'ghosts' they are. Recently, my master became so desperate that he offered a handsome reward to anyone who could rid the castle of this plague."

"And you expect to accomplish it with this owl?" asked the circus man.

"Indeed I do," said the gardener, and after a little bargaining they agreed on a price.

The gardener stowed the cage in his cart and set out; he had a long trek across the countryside before reaching the castle.

The owl was hot and sleepy, riding along under the warm sun.

"Where are we going this time?" she wondered, "and where are all the other animals and the people who bring me my food? Why is no one coming to feed me?"

"This will put an end to the mouse plague," the gardener was thinking. He rubbed his hands in anticipation of the reward, for he knew he was the only one to understand that the unsettling noises in the night were made by a large family of mice.

When he reached the castle, he took the cage to the attic and opened it, and the bewildered owl took refuge in an old wardrobe.

At nightfall the mice came out of their holes and started playing. They ran and scratched, whistled and nibbled, and were having a merry time, when suddenly—

they discovered the white owl in her hiding place, and scampered, terrified, back into their mouseholes. They thought they had seen a ghost. Not a sound could be heard in the whole castle, and everyone at last enjoyed a good night's sleep. In the morning a grateful master bestowed the reward.

Alas, the peace and quiet were of short duration. The very next night, the owl began feeling lonely, and, worse, was growing very hungry, as no one had brought her any food. So, finally, she took a deep breath and let out a loud "Whooooooo-Whooooooo!"

The frightening, eerie sound travelled down the flues and, through the fireplace, straight into the bedroom where the master and lady were sleeping. They got such a shock that they almost fell out of bed. "A ghost, a spirit, a monster!" they shrieked, pale and shivering.

Only one little mouse who heard that call thought she recognized someone lonely and hungry. She slipped out of her hiding place and, seeing the great bird in the closet, gathered all her courage and asked, "Are you a ghost?"

"Of course not," said the owl. "I am a bird. I belonged to the circus—"

"What is a circus?" asked the mouse.

"It is a big round house that moves around the country," said the owl. "It is a strange existence. When the sun shines and I am sleepy, humans come and stand behind bars to talk about me. They make a lot of noise or badger me with little sticks, but it is worse at night, when I'm wide awake; that is when I feel lonely."

"That must be awful," said the brave mouse sympathetically. "I have never been lonely. We are such a large family. But I have always wanted to fly. Out there, the night sky is so beautiful and wide. It must be fantastic to soar with your wings spread wide. Is it?"

"How would I know?" said the owl. "I cannot fly. I cannot remember ever flying. I am trapped here now."

"Oh, dear," said the little mouse. "Let me think about it. There must be something that can be done!"

The next morning the weary master, with the loud hoots still ringing in his ears, went to find the gardener. "You helped us get rid of that earlier trouble. Please try again," he said, taking three gold coins from his pocket. "The scratches and whistles and little squeals were nothing compared to the monstrous howls that new ghost was emitting last night!"

"I will do my best," said the gardener, "and I will begin right away."

Quietly he slipped up to the attic and opened a window.

The day passed and the evening came again; the moon was lighting up the sky, and the mouse had come back and was admiring the owl.

"How thrilling to have wings, like you," she said wistfully. Just as she spoke, they felt a draft of fresh air, and realized that the window was wide open. How sweet the night air smelled! At last, a chance—

"Take courage, be brave," cried the little mouse. The owl hesitated. Then she hopped up to the windowsill, spread her mighty wings and flew off into the night sky.

And on her back, with a pounding heart, rode the little mouse.

Once again there were scratches, squeals, whistles and a hundred tiny feet running all over the castle attic each night.

"It sounds almost cosy, don't you think, my dear?" remarked the master to his wife.

"Indeed," she replied. "I had become so used to the noises that I almost missed them when they stopped."

And the owl? The owl lived in freedom to a ripe old age.